Twinkle, Twinkle, Little Lamb

To Mary and Frankie Brewster —B.H.

For Keaton xx —S.J.

Text copyright © 2018 Bridget Heos • Illustrations copyright © Sarah Jennings
Published in 2018 by Amicus Ink, an imprint of Amicus • P.O. Box 1329 • Mankato, MN 56002 • www.amicuspublishing.us

Library of Congress Cataloging-in-Publication Data
Names: Heos, Bridget, author. | Jennings, Sarah, illustrator.
Title: Twinkle, twinkle, little lamb / by Bridget Heos ; illustrated by Sarah Jennings.
Description: Mankato, MN : Amicus Ink, [2018] | Summary: Mary mixes up the words of "Twinkle,
Twinkle, Little Star" with "Mary Had a Little Lamb," which pleases the star but not the lamb.
Identifiers: LCCN 2017049006 | ISBN 9781681524054 (hardcover)
Subjects: | CYAC: Nursery rhymes—Fiction. | Stars—Fiction. | Sheep—Fiction. |
Animals—Infancy—Fiction. | Humorous stories.
Classification: LCC PZ7.H4118 Twi 2018 | DDC [E]--dc23
LC record available at https://lccn.loc.gov/2017049006

Editor: Rebecca Glaser
Designer: Kathleen Petelinsek

First edition 9 8 7 6 5 4 3 2 1 • Printed in China

Twinkle, Twinkle, Little Lamb

BY BRIDGET HEOS · ILLUSTRATED BY SARAH JENNINGS

amicus ink

Mankato, Minnesota

Twinkle, twinkle, little

Lamb,

How I wonder what you—

WAIT!
You're mixed up. It should be "Mary had a little," not "Twinkle, twinkle, little."

little star, little star,
Mary had a little star...

whose fleece was white as snow.

NO, NO!
That's not right, either.
My fleece is white as snow.
Star twinkles.

Up above the world so high,
like a diamond in the sky.

Very funny.

Star, tell her you belong up here instead of me.

I don't know what
you're talking about.
I belong right here, as
Mary's beloved pet.

Twinkle, twinkle, little lamb.

How I wonder,
how I wonder,
how I wonder…

It's not **SUPPOSED** to rhyme with lamb.
I'm not **SUPPOSED** to be in this song.
I'm the **LAMB** in Mary Had a Little Lamb!
It's little lamb, little lamb!

Whose fleece was pink as ham? Hmm . . . that does have a nice ring to it.

It followed her to school one day,
school one day,
school one day.

NO, NO!
I make the children laugh and play, laugh and play, laugh and play!
Not Star!
I don't know. I'm a pretty fun guy.

Mary had a little lamb,
little lamb, little lamb . . .

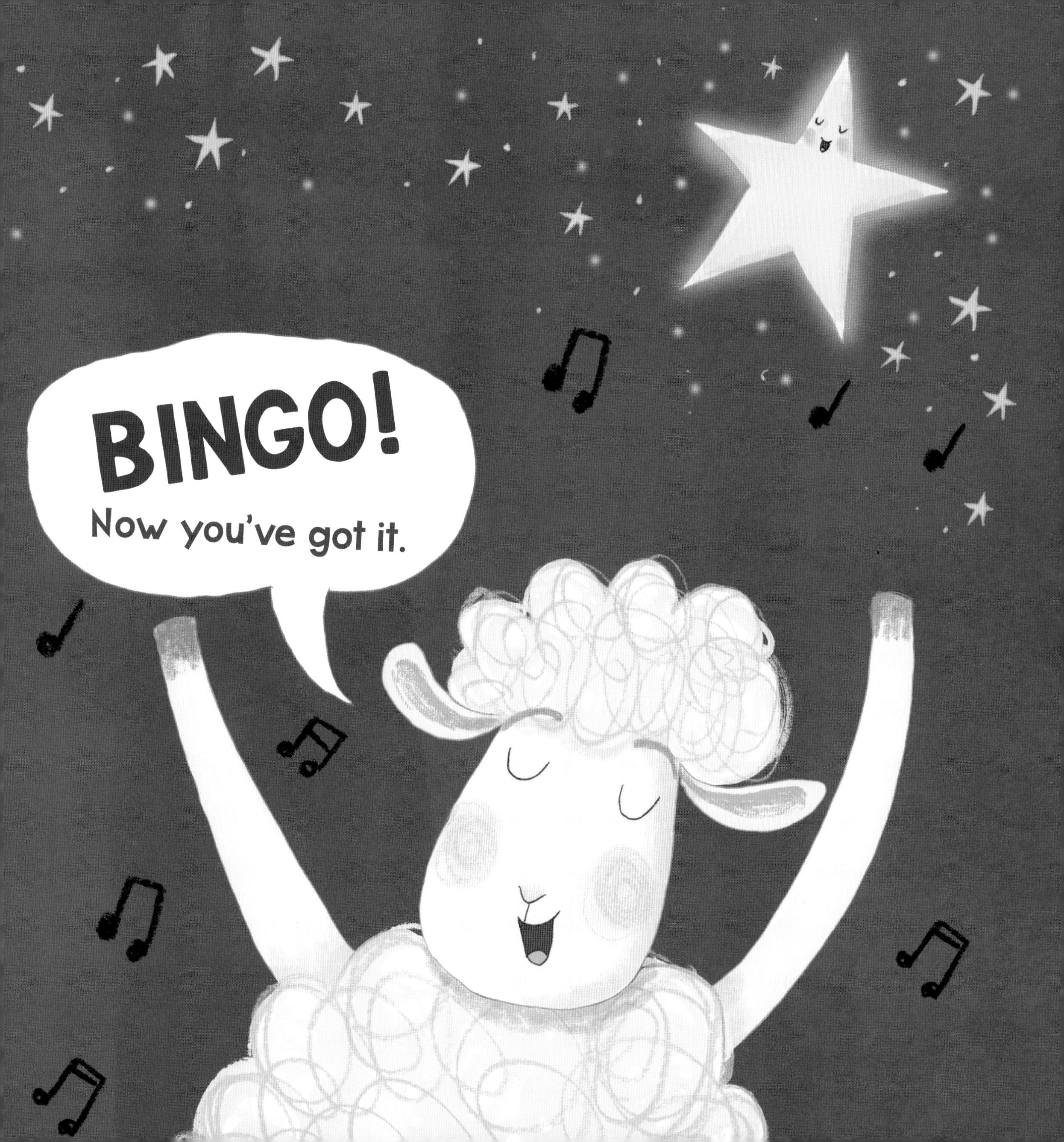
BINGO!
Now you've got it.

The wheels on the **lamb** go round and round...